Dear Family,

What's the best way to help your child love reading?

Find good books like this one to share—and read together!

Here are some tips.

●**Take a "picture walk."** Look at all the pictures before you read. Talk about what you see.

●**Take turns.** Read to your child. Ham it up! Use different voices for different characters, and read with feeling! Then listen as your child reads to you, or explains the story in his or her own words.

●**Point out words as you read.** Help your child notice how letters and sounds go together. Point out unusual or difficult words that your child might not know. Talk about those words and what they mean.

●**Ask questions.** Stop to ask questions as you read. For example: "What do you think will happen next?" "How would you feel if that happened to you?"

●**Read every day.** Good stories are worth reading more than once! Read signs, labels, and even cereal boxes with your child. Visit the library to take out more books. And look for other JUST FOR YOU! BOOKS you and your child can share!

The Editors

To Leah Alexis Hudson — CWH

To my son Scott and my new daughter-in-law Armia,
who make my heart sing — SW

Library of Congress Cataloging-in-Publication Data

Hudson, Cheryl Willis.
    What do you know? : snow! / by Cheryl Willis Hudson ; illustrated by Sylvia Walker.
    p. cm.—(Just for You! Level 2)
    Summary: On a snowy Saturday, Sydney is excited to be the first one on her street
to go outside, and she has even more fun when her brother joins her in scooping,
crunching, packing, and playing in the snow. Includes activity ideas for parents
and children.
    ISBN 0-439-56851-X (pbk.)
    [1.Snow—Fiction. 2. Play—Fiction. 3. Brothers and sisters—Fiction. 4. African
Americans—Fiction.] I. Walker, Sylvia, ill. II. Title. III. Series.

PZ7.H8656Wh 2004
[E]—dc22
                                                                2004042911

10 9 8 7 6 5 4 3 2 1   04 05 06 07 08
        Printed in the U.S.A. 23 • First Scholastic Printing, February 2004

What Do You Know?
SNOW!

by Cheryl Willis Hudson
Illustrated by Sylvia Walker

JUST FOR YOU!™
Level 2

Sydney woke up early one Saturday.
She smiled and stretched.
"What will I do today?"
she asked herself.

Sydney peeked out of her window.
She looked down at the street.
"What do you know?" said
Sydney. "Snow!"

There was no snow on the ground
last night.
Sydney checked before her mother
switched off her light.

But now a soft, white blanket
covered the hard, gray concrete.
Snow covered everything from
trash cans to streetlights.

The sun was just coming up.
Sydney wanted to be the first one
on her block to play in the fresh
clean snow.
She washed up,
pulled on her pants,
tied up her boots,
slipped on her jacket,
and grabbed her hat and mittens.

Quietly Sydney tiptoed out
of her apartment.
Her mom blew her a kiss.

Outside on the front stoop,
Sydney took a deep breath.
She blew out the air.
It came out of her mouth
in white puffs like smoke.
Oh, it was cold!

Sydney looked around.
She was the first one outside.
Her boots made big tracks
in her front yard.
Sydney saw gray smoke rising
from the chimneys.

She saw snow piled on the streetlights
like ice cream cones.
She saw icicles dripping from the iron
fences.
She picked up a handful of snow
and threw it.

Sydney smiled to herself.
"This is fun," she said, "but it
would be more fun if I had
someone to play with."
That's when her little brother,
Brandon, came running
down the stairs!
"What can we do with the snow?"
he asked Sydney.

They scooped it, carried it,
smashed it, and rolled it.

They stomped it, crunched it,
packed it, and molded it.

They swept it, shaped it,
held it, and stacked it.

That's what they did with the snow.

Suddenly a slow-moving snow
plow appeared.
Foot by foot it pushed small
hills of snow toward the curb.
"Wow!" Sydney said to Brandon.
"It looks like the white blanket
is being pulled off the street!"

Soon Sydney saw Mrs. Scott
waving from her window.
Mr. Smith came out with a shovel.
He started to clean the sidewalk
in front of his store.

A bus pulled up to the bus stop.
Shoppers and workers got off.
They tried not to slip on the
slippery sidewalk.
A big boy rolled a cart toward
the Laundromat.
Sister Nandi turned on the
lights in her beauty shop.

Sydney smiled
to herself.
Playing in the snow
made her feel all
warm inside.

Outside, her fingers
and toes were
tingling.

Brandon was
shivering from
the cold.

Sydney took one last
look at her front yard.

Then she opened her arms wide
and called out to her neighbors.
"What do you know?" she shouted.
"Snow!"
Everyone smiled and waved.

Sydney put her arm around
her little brother.
They ran upstairs to their apartment,
and what do you know?

Mom was waiting
to warm them up
with oatmeal and
hot chocolate
for breakfast.

Here are some fun things for you to do.

YOU Are There!

The author and artist make you feel as if YOU are out in the snow with Sydney!

Use your words to tell about being out in the snow.

What would it feel like to walk on the snowy street?

What would it feel like to touch the snow?

How would you feel if a snow plow came and pushed the snow away?

Look back in the story to page 18.
The author says the children **scooped** the snow.

What other special words does she use to tell about what they did with it? ▲

What would YOU do with the snow? Make a list using YOUR words.

▲ carried, smashed, rolled, stomped, crunched, packed, molded, swept, shaped, held, and stacked.

YOUR Snowman

If you had a lot of snow,
YOU could build a snowman,
too. What else would
you need, besides snow?

Now think:
What would you do first?
What would you do second?
What would you do third?
What would you do last?

Write four sentences to tell how you would build
YOUR snowman. Draw pictures to go with your words.
Remember to give your snowman a hat!

▲▲▲▲TOGETHER TIME ▲▲▲▲

*Make some time to share ideas about the story with your young reader!
Here are some activities you can try. There are no right or wrong
answers.*

Think About It: Ask your child, "Why do you think the author
picked the title *What Do You Know? Snow!* for her story? Can you
think of another good title for this book?"

Talk About It: What is winter like where you live? Talk about it
with your child. What do you each like about the winter? What
DON'T you like about it?

Read More: What else does your child want to know about
snow? Visit the library to find more books about snow and winter
weather.

Meet the Author

CHERYL WILLIS HUDSON says, "Snow rarely fell during the winters in my childhood town of Portsmouth, Virginia. When it did, the snow melted so quickly that my brothers and I felt cheated because we could barely scoop up enough to make snowballs. As an adult living in New Jersey, I see snow every winter. Still, I am amazed by how fresh snow looks and feels. Unlike me, my son and daughter played in snow as high as 18 inches! Everyone seems to love that fluffy, cold stuff—especially children."

Cheryl Willis Hudson is the author of many picture books for children, including *Hands Can!; AFRO-BETS® ABC Book; Come By Here, Lord;* and *Bright Eyes, Brown Skin,* which she co-authored with Bernette Ford. Cheryl and her husband Wade are the founders of Just Us Books, Inc., a small press that specializes in publishing Black-interest books for children.

Meet the Artist

SYLVIA WALKER says, "My family and I are from California. While my children were young, they never experienced snow. When we moved east and they finally did see snow, they were thrilled. Just like the boy and girl in the story, they couldn't wait to go out and play in the snow. Of course, they always came back indoors freezing from the cold."

Sylvia is a native of Pasadena, California, and now lives in Philadelphia, Pennsylvania. She studied at the California Institute of Arts in Los Angeles and earned a Bachelor of Fine Arts degree. Sylvia uses water color, pencil, ink, and acrylic to create her artwork. Her works include paintings on canvas, children's fashion illustration, as well as many children's books for Just Us Books, Scholastic, and others.